W9-BIG-622

This book
belongs to:

Text written by Gill Davies/Illustrated by Tina Freeman
First published in Great Britain in 2001 by Brimax
an imprint of Octopus Publishing Group Ltd
2-4 Heron Quays, London, E14 4JP
© Octopus Publishing Group Ltd

Happy Hen

BRIMAX READ WITH ME

Happy Hen

It is morning on Yellow Barn Farm.

The cockerel crows, the cows moo,
the pigs oink, and the lambs baa.
It is very noisy!

"Sshhhh!" says Happy Hen. "My
eggs are sleeping." Then she sits
down and sings a song to her eggs.

That night, Happy Hen whispers to her eggs.

"Yellow Barn Farm is a wonderful place. Soon you will hatch. Then you will be able to see for yourselves."

And then Happy Hen sings a lullaby to her sleepy eggs before she falls asleep, too.

The next morning it is time for the eggs to hatch.

Peck! Peck! Peck! Ten little beaks break open the shells.

Squeak! Squeak! Squeak! Ten little chicks tumble out.

"Welcome to Yellow Barn Farm," moos Mrs Cow, who has come to see the chicks.

Soon the little chicks are scampering and flapping all over the farmyard.

"Squeak! Squeak! Squeak!" they all chirp happily.

"Oink! Oink! Oink!" says a happy piglet to the chicks.

The chicks follow their mother everywhere, and copy everything she does.

Happy Hen laughs... so do ten little chicks.

Happy Hen dances... so do ten little chicks – but three fall over!

And when Happy Hen sings, ten little chicks sing, too.

And now, every morning, all the farm animals sing songs.

The cockerel crows, Mrs Cow moos, the little piglets oink, and Lucy Lamb baas.

And Happy Hen clucks and chirps with her ten little chicks.

And every night, all the animals sing lullabies.

The mice squeak, the owls hoot, and the cats miaow.

And Happy Hen tweets and twitters with her ten little chicks.

Yellow Barn Farm is even noisier than ever, but now it is full of songs and lullabies.

Farmer Jones looks around at his farm and smiles to himself.

What a happy Yellow Barn Farm this is!

Here are some words in the story. Can you read them?

farm	eggs
cockerel	chicks
cows	farmyard
pigs	mice
piglets	owls
lambs	cats
hen	farmer

How much of the story can you remember?

What does the cockerel do in the morning on Yellow Barn Farm?

What are the eggs doing at the beginning of the story?

What does Happy Hen sing to her eggs before she falls asleep?

What tumbles out of the eggs?

Is Yellow Barn Farm noisy?

Who looks around the farm and smiles?

Read with me in words and pictures

Happy Hen lives in a  .

Every morning the  crows,

the  moo,

the  oink

and the  baa!

Happy Hen has ten  .

Soon the eggs hatch into  .

The  flap all

over the  .

At night the  is very noisy.

The squeak, the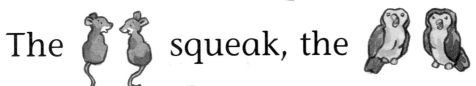

hoot and the  miaow!

Notes for parents

The Yellow Barn Farm stories will help to expand your child's vocabulary and reading skills.

Key words are listed in each of the books and are repeated several times - point them out along with the corresponding illustrations as you read the story. The following ideas for discussion will expand on the things your child has read and learnt about on the farm, and will make the experience of reading more pleasurable.

• Talk about the many different noises and sounds that you can hear on Yellow Barn Farm in the morning. Make the different animal sounds and ask your child to point to the animal that they think makes the sound in the illustrations.

• Talk about all the sounds on Yellow Barn Farm at night. Can you hear any owls hooting or cats miaowing near your home at night? If possible relate the animals and objects seen in Yellow Barn Farm to real animals and objects in your child's daily life. Point them out to your child so they can bridge the gap between books and reality, which will help to make books all the more real!